OVER THE RIVER AND THROUGH THE WOODS

Illustrations copyright © 1992 by John Gurney.

All rights reserved. Published by Scholastic Inc. SCHOLASTIC, CARTWHEEL BOOKS,
and associated logos are trademarks and/or registered trademarks of Scholastic Inc.

12 11 10 9 8 7 6 5 4 3 2 1   5 6 7 8 9/0

Printed in Singapore   46

This edition created exclusively for Barnes & Noble, Inc.

2005 Barnes & Noble Books

ISBN 0-7607-9588-6

This edition first printing, October 2005

OVER THE RIVER AND THROUGH THE WOODS

Illustrated by John Steven Gurney

SCHOLASTIC INC.

New York Toronto London Auckland Sydney
Mexico City New Delhi Hong Kong Buenos Aires

I would like to thank Mom, Dad, Phyllis, Brian, Lauren, and Steven for posing; Linda Barclay and family for use of the sleigh; the Mercer Museum for their historical assistance; and Patty Anne, Brian, and Christopher for the cameo with the snowman.

To the warmth and comfort of Thanksgiving, to my parents for providing it, and, as always, to Kathie.

— J. S. G.

Over the river and through the woods,
To Grandmother's house we go.

The horse knows the way
to carry the sleigh

Through the white and drifted snow.

Over the river and through the woods,
Oh, how the wind does blow!

It stings the toes
and bites the nose,

As over the ground we go.

Over the river and through the woods,
Trot fast, my dapple gray!

Spring over the ground
like a hunting hound,
For this is Thanksgiving Day.

Over the river and through the woods,
Now Grandfather's face I spy!

Hurrah for the fun!

Is the turkey done?

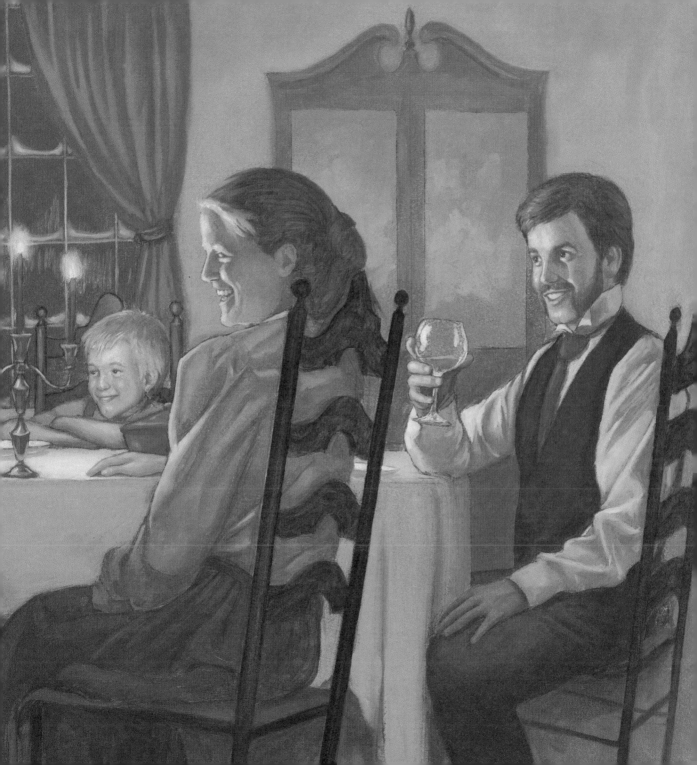

Hurrah for the pumpkin pie!

Over the River and Through the Woods